Blue's Big Parade!

by Justin Spelvin
illustrated by Ian Chernichaw

Simon Spotlight/Nick Jr.
New York   London   Toronto   Sydney

Based on the TV series *Blue's Clues*® created by Traci Paige Johnson,
Todd Kessler, and Angela C. Santomero as seen on Nick Jr.®
On *Blue's Clues*, Joe is played by Donovan Patton. Photos by Joan Marcus.

 SIMON SPOTLIGHT
An imprint of Simon & Schuster Children's Publishing Division
1230 Avenue of the Americas, New York, New York 10020
Copyright © 2005 Viacom International Inc. All rights reserved. NICKELODEON, NICK JR.,
Blue's Clues, and all related titles, logos, and characters are registered trademarks of Viacom
International Inc.
Manufactured in the United States of America
10 9 8 7 6 5
ISBN 0-689-87673-4

Summer had arrived. Blue and her friends were all excited about the town's big summer celebration.

"I have an idea to make this the best summer celebration ever," Blue told her friends. "We could have our very own parade!"

"Great idea, Blue!" said Joe excitedly. "Everyone loves a parade!"

"Peri-perfect! But there's so much to do!" said Periwinkle.

"I know how we can do it all," Blue answered cheerfully. "We can work together."

They all agreed to get started first thing the next morning.

The next day Tickety brought out a calendar. "The celebration is on Saturday, and today is Monday. That means we have five days until our summertime parade."

"First we need some instruments," Blue said to her friends.

"But where can we find instruments?" asked Mr. Salt.

Monday	Tuesday	Wednesday	Thursday	Friday	Saturday

"Look out!" warned Mrs. Pepper, but it was too late. Mr. Salt bumped into a pot on the counter. It fell to the floor with a *CLANG!*
"Hey," said Blue. "That gives me an idea!"

"We can use pots and pans as our instruments!" Blue suggested.

So they each grabbed a pot or a pan and gave it a *BANG* with a spoon. The kitchen filled with the sound of all their bang-bang-banging.

"All together now!" cheered Mrs. Pepper. And they each banged in rhythm.

"We sound like a real marching band!" Periwinkle called out over the drumming.

At the end of the day Tickety crossed off Monday from the calendar.

Five minus one leaves four days left.

Monday	Tuesday	Wednesday	Thursday	Friday	Saturday
X					

"Today we can make the floats," Blue announced the next morning.

"All good parades have floats!" Magenta agreed. "But how can we make them?"

Just then Green Puppy pulled in a wagon full of supplies.

"Hey, I've got it!" Magenta exclaimed.

"Wagons!" Magenta said. "We can use wagons to make the floats!"

"Yeah!" said Blue. "Wagons are just what we need!"

"And I have cardboard, cloth, and ribbons to help build them," Green Puppy added.

For the rest of the afternoon Blue and her friends had a terrific time turning three regular wagons into three *terrific* summertime floats!

Three days left!

Monday	Tuesday	Wednesday	Thursday	Friday	Saturday
X	X				

"Let's get party hats to wear to the parade," Joe suggested the next day.

"But where will we find party hats?" asked
Purple Kangaroo.

"Maybe we could make and decorate our own hats!" Blue said.
"Yeah! We can put our favorite things about summer on them,"
Magenta suggested.

"Then they'll be super-duper summer hats," Joe agreed.

So they all cut and taped and showed off their favorite things about summer.

Two days left, everyone!

Monday	Tuesday	Wednesday	Thursday	Friday	Saturday
X	X	X			

The next morning everyone was excited about marching practice. Except things didn't go well at all!

"March left!" said March-leader Blue. But everyone marched to the right.

"Now march right!" called Blue. But everyone marched to the left.

"Now stop!" Blue shouted. But the back of the line kept marching . . . and everyone fell in a big pile!

"That wasn't peri-perfect," said a nervous Periwinkle.
"Don't worry," said Blue. "We just need more practice."

We still have one more day left!

Monday	Tuesday	Wednesday	Thursday	Friday	Saturday
X	X	X	X		⚑

The next day marching practice went better. "Just follow me," Blue called out to the group. "Left. Right. Left. Right . . ."

They followed. Left. Right. Left. Right. And soon enough they were marching together!

"We're doing it!" said Periwinkle happily.

"That's great!" cheered Blue. "Now let's bang our drums."
They banged in time and marched all around the backyard.

Tomorrow is the big day!

Monday	Tuesday	Wednesday	Thursday	Friday	Saturday
X	X	X	X	X	

"Happy summertime!" Blue and her friends cheered as they marched down the street the next day. They banged their drums and waved to the happy crowd.

The parade was a big hit! Blue led them all through town.

The crowd whistled, cheered, and applauded.
It was the perfect way to celebrate summer!

That night the whole town watched as fireworks lit up the sky.

"Happy summer, Blue!" Joe said.

"Happy summer, EVERYONE," Blue answered happily.